All inquiries should be addressed to:
Barron's Educational Series, Inc.
250 Wireless Boulevard
Hauppauge, NY 11788

International Standard Book No. 0-7641-0001-7

Library of Congress Catalog Card No. 96-84984

Printed and bound in Belgium by Proust N.V.

First published in Great Britain in 1996
by Macdonald Young Books
61 Western Road
Hove
East Sussex
BN3 1JD

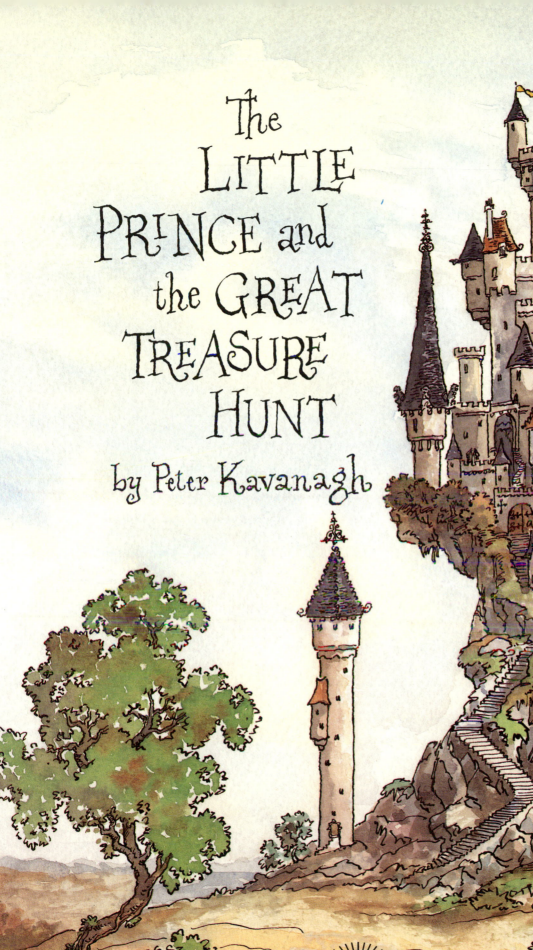

The
LITTLE
PRINCE and
the GREAT
TREASURE
HUNT

by Peter Kavanagh

BARRON'S

Hi! I'm the Little Prince and this is my friend, Teddy.
We're visiting Uncle King John and Aunty Queen Mary.

What a dump this castle is! Not as good as our castle.

You're right, Little Prince.
Our castle is not as good as yours—
it's much better!

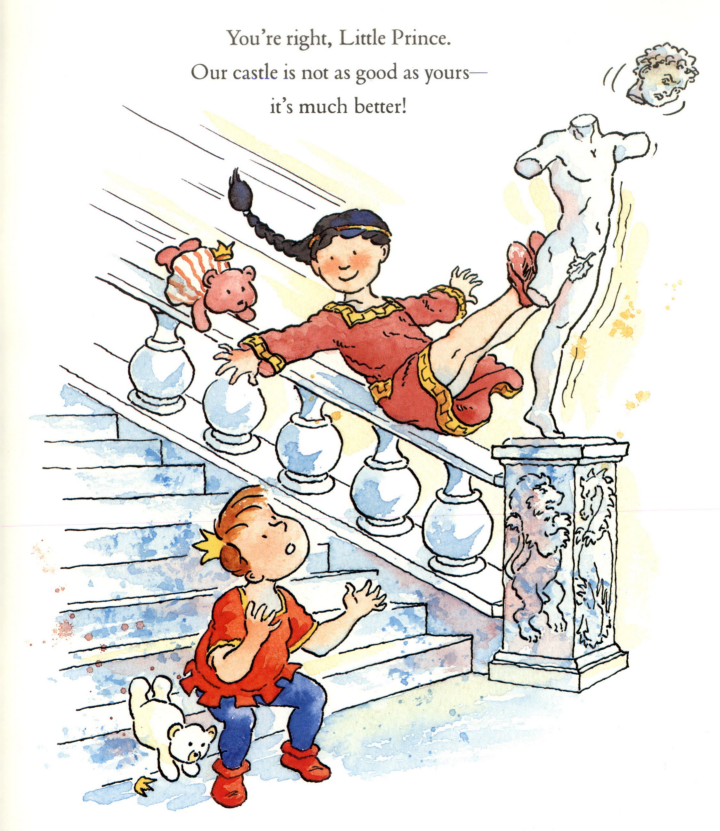

Oh no, it's the Little Princess and her bear, Cuddly. They're girls.

I bet your silly old castle doesn't have moaning, groaning ghosts?

Yes it does.

I bet it doesn't have secret, creepy passages?

Yes it does.

I bet it doesn't have dark, gloomy dungeons?

Yes it does.

Well I bet it doesn't have hidden, buried treasure.

Er . . . no . . . it doesn't. Does yours?

Maybe it does and maybe it doesn't, but I'm not showing you!

Quick, Teddy—after her!

2 Short cut to door 7

3 Dead End

5 Short cut to door 3

6 Short cut to door 5

To the Moat

8 Short cut to door 4

OK, Little Princess, where is the buried treasure?

Are you sure you're brave enough to find out?

After all, you're only boys.

Teddy and I can face anything together. Can't we, Teddy?

We will have to ask the Old Woman of the Wood. Read these rules and hope the wolf doesn't catch you!

CRY WOLF

A game to get you through the woods...

Play with two or more people using a die and counters. Each player rolls the die to move around the squares. Follow any instructions you land on:

Anyone who throws a five becomes the wolf and chases everyone. If the wolf lands on your counter you're caught. Go to the wolf's den. Take your turn with the die but you cannot move until the wolf is caught. (Only one wolf at a time.)

The wolf is caught when anyone, except the wolf, throws a one. The wolf is now a player again and continues the game from the den.

The game is over when somebody reaches the Old Woman's cottage and the story can continue.

THROW 6
To START

FOLLOW
ARROW

FOLLOW
ARROW

FOLLOW
ARROW

WOLF'S DEN

STOP! THROW ODD NUMBER TO CROSS

STOP! THROW EVEN NUMBER TO CROSS

THE END

STOP! THROW ODD NUMBER TO CROSS

FOLLOW ARROW

GO BACK 6

Hello, children,
have you come for tea?
You do look delicious.

No, Old Woman of the Wood. We've come to
ask you where we can find the hidden treasure
in King John's castle.

And what will you give me, children, in return for my answer?
Will you give me your teddy bears for my collection?

No, we love our teddies too much.
Come on Little Princess, let's go home.

Wait, children, you are right! A good teddy is worth
more than any hidden treasure.
But I cannot help you unless you bring back my five
golden rings from the Naiads in the lake.

Can you swim, Little Prince?

Like a frog, Little Princess.

Now I can reach up to get you this key. You must seek the Laughing Doors in the castle. Beyond the door that this key opens, you will find the treasure hidden in a small, wooden chest.

Thank you, Old…er…Young Woman of the Wood.
OK, let's get back to the castle!

What goes through a door without opening it? Your voice!
Who's at the door? *It's the Little Frog Prince.* Tell him to hop it!
What goes creak, creak, ha, ha, slam? A laughing door!
What did the Little Princess say when she saw all these doors? Look at all these doors!

Who's at the door? *The Invisible Man.* Tell him I can't see him!

I'd tell you another door joke but you'd only tell me to shut it.

What should you do if you open a door and find a dragon behind it? Shut it again!

This is it—the treasure room!
Stop laughing everyone and come on.

It's my castle so I get to open the chest.
OK, OK! What's inside?

It's a little, golden dragon...and it's alive!

And I fly, Little Princess.

Am I not a wonderful treasure to have found?

But tell me this, is it not more wonderful

to have a treasure yet to find?

So follow me back through the book,
and hunt again for a dragon
hidden on every page.

Come on, everyone!
Back to the beginning!